Foxy

in the kitchen

Colin and Jacqui Hawkins

Collins

An Imprint of HarperCollinsPublishers

Foxy and his little sister decided to make some cakes for tea. "I like rock cakes," said Foxy.

In the kitchen they set to work. "I've got the sugar," said Foxy's little sister.

"Ooops!" Foxy dropped the flour.

"I've got the butter," said Foxy's little sister.
Craaack! Foxy dropped the eggs.

"Whoops!" cried Foxy as the

milk flew from his paws.

Then they put everything into a large bowl and mixed it all up together.
"I like cooking," said Foxy.

"And I like stirring," said his little sister.

Foxy dropped the cake mixture in blobs on the tray. "They do look like rocks," said his little sister.

Very carefully Foxy put the
cakes into the hot oven.
"Yummy," said his
little sister as she
licked the spoon.

Foxy and his little sister did the washing up. They had lots of fun splashing and sploshing in the soapsuds.

"Oh! No!" cried Foxy. "I can smell burning."

And he ran to the oven.

But it was too late. The cakes were very burnt.
"Hello!" said Dog.
"What's cooking?"
"Would you like a lolly?" asked Badger.

"Yuk! Your cakes do taste like rocks," said Badger.
"Well, I like them," said Dog.
"They're very crunchy."

And he munched them all up.
"I must do more cooking,"
laughed Foxy.

First published in Great Britain by HarperCollins Publishers Ltd in 1995. ISBN 0 00 198148 X (hardback) 10 9 8 7 6 5 4 3 2 1
ISBN 0 00 664539 9 (paperback) 10 9 8 7 6 5 4 3 2 1 Text and illustrations copyright © Colin and Jacqui Hawkins 1995.
Printed and bound in Italy.